CAROLINE

Brandi Carlile

Lyrics written by
Brandi Carlile

Used by permission from Southern Oracle Music (ASCAP)
and WB Music Corp.

"Caroline"
By Brandi M. Carlile, Timothy Jay Hanseroth and Phillip John Hanseroth
WB Music Corp. (ASCAP) and Southern Oracle Music LLC (ASCAP)
All Rights Administered By WB Music Corp.

ISBN: 978-0-938120-7-4

First published in 2014 by Huqua Press
An operating division of Morling Manor Corporation
Los Angeles, California

Illustrated by Yoko Matsuoko
Graphic Design: designSimple

www.huquapress.com

A firm believer that artists in the public eye have a social and moral responsibility to promote and marry humanitarian efforts with their musical agenda, Brandi Carlile founded The Looking Out Foundation in 2008. The foundation serves the chronically underserved through its ongoing philanthropic efforts and involvement with social issues.

lookingoutfoundation.org

Printed in the United States of America

VICTORIA, JESSICA, DAVID, MICHAEL, JASON, ALEXANDER, CASI AND BRIANNA. THEY ARE MY "CAROLINES."

My nieces and nephews. When I travel the world and visit far-flung places, I imagine seeing remarkable vistas through their eyes. I send postcards. Bring trinkets for them. And share stories of teaching a Massai warrior yoga in Kenya or cuddling a monkey in Panama. I convey the wonder of being in Haiti and witnessing the resiliency of its people so soon after decimation. The joy of being atop the Spanish Steps in Rome on New Year's Eve or spying a bear in Alaska. Gawking as floating lanterns gracefully ascend to the sky in Chiang Mai. Hiking in remote Patagonia with air so pure you tingle all over. Traveling the once tiny footsteps of their great-grandmother in Poland. Watching wolf cubs play in northern Idaho. Or standing in the remote bush in Australia, surrounded by kangaroos. All the while, thinking of them. Missing them. And hoping they too can one day experience the magic and majesty in earth's nooks and crannies. And they are. David has navigated the world with his band and Jessica, the newlywed, is already an intrepid traveler.

Hurling through the clouds to some remarkable destination is one of my greatest passions. Preceded only by my love for family, friends and animals. Brandi's "Caroline" captures the conflict that these journeys bring. A great big thrill to be in the moment of it all. A joy to share it with those we love. And twinges of missing who and what we leave behind as we wander and explore.

I was first introduced to Brandi's music by my niece Jessica. We were on one of our Saturday afternoon adventures when she popped a CD into my car's player, saying "You'll love this song." It was *The Story*. She was right. I did love it. I listened to it again and again. And again. I teared up every time. I've seen Brandi perform the song twice in concert, and both times I wept. Such depth of emotion.

When I decided to publish illustrated books based on meaningful songs for my Huqua Press, I knew I would want Brandi Carlile to be among the first. Brandi guided me to *Caroline*, and its lyrics, music and Elton John vocals on the track were inspiring and exactly what I had in mind.

The song is an anthem for those we leave behind. But even more it's a reminder that when we love profoundly and purely we never really leave our little (and big) loves tethered. They're with us always, and knowing that makes the journey all the more spectacular. And in *Caroline*, Brandi reminds the children, grandchildren, nieces and nephews that no matter where work and life lead us – no matter what form the wanderlust call takes – you're in our hearts, always.

Judith A. Proffer
Founder, Huqua Press

I WOKE UP
LONG AFTER DAWN

20 YEARS HAD COME AND GONE

I KNOW WHEN IT
CHANGED FOR ME

A DAY IN JUNE
YOU CAME TO ME

BELIZE
PASSPORT
FRANCE
1861
DESTINATIONS
TURKEY
33.50
№ 38882/08
ad345678

I've seen through someone else's eyes
With nothin' on the other side
Every motel, every town
Pieces scattered all around

PROMISES
THAT I CAN'T BE
SOMEONE'S
HEART
THAT I CAN'T KEEP

DAYS SO LONG
I COULDN'T SPEAK

ROADS SO
ROCKY

I CAN'T SLEEP

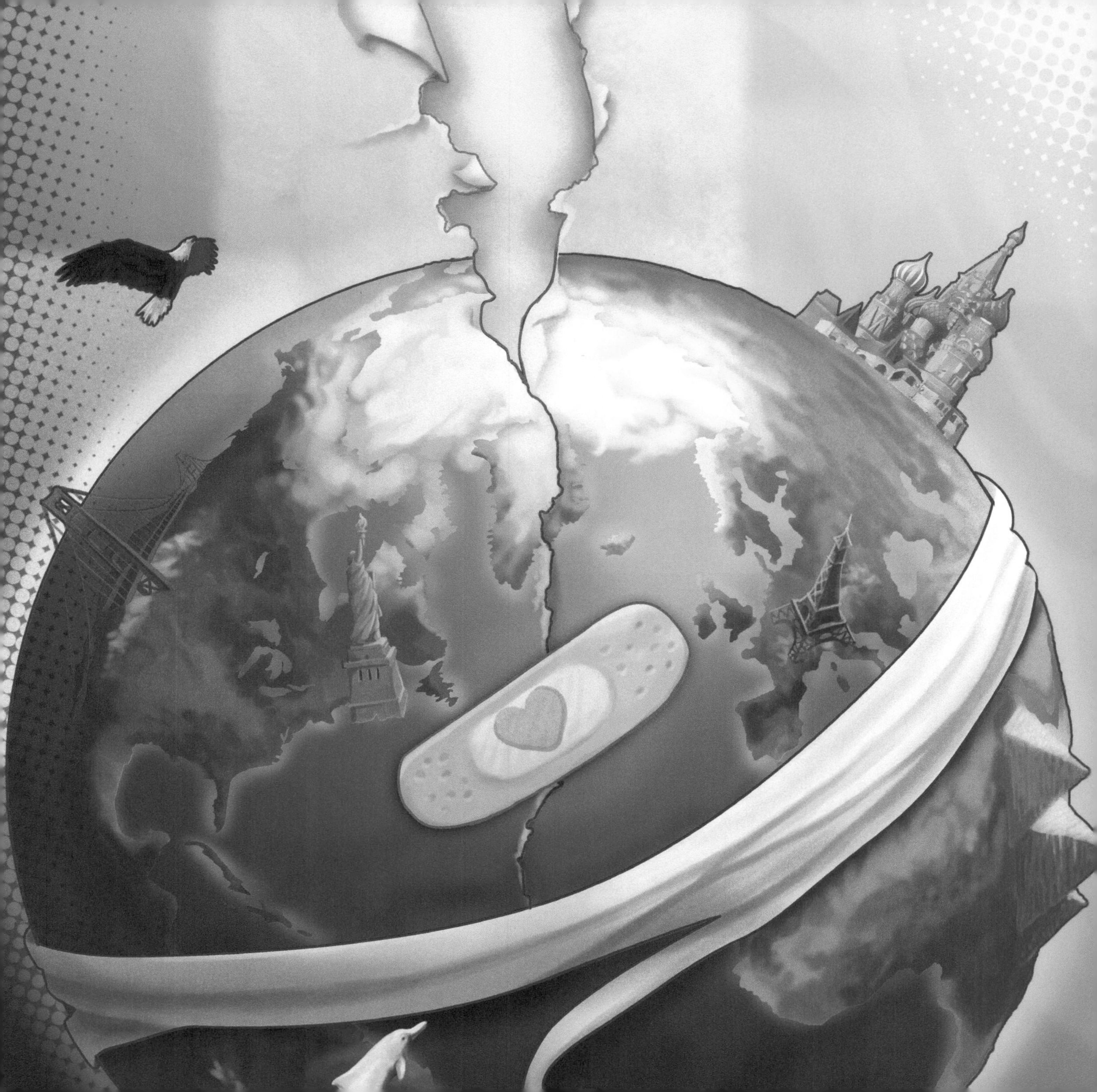

But I've seen things
so beautiful
All around this
broken world
that pale
in comparison to you

CAROLINE

I'M ON MY WAY
BACK HOME TO YOU

CAN'T IMAGINE

WHAT I'M GOIN' THROUGH
WITHOUT YOU BY MY SIDE

IT'S BEEN A
LONG, LONG TIME

CAROLINE
BRANDI

Oh, won't you say a prayer for me
I hope you will remember me
You're always on my mind

I HAVE SEEN
THE CANYON LANDS

CROOKED LINES LIKE IN YOUR HANDS

YOU'D SWEAR
THE EARTH WAS
SPLIT IN TWO

I WOULDN'T LIE I PROMISE YOU

THAT I HAVE SEEN IT,
YOU WILL, TOO
YOU COULD NOT BELIEVE
IF NOT FOR
PHOTOGRAPHS
I TOOK FOR YOU,
CAROLINE

They've built towers to the sky
It hurts sometimes
to watch them try

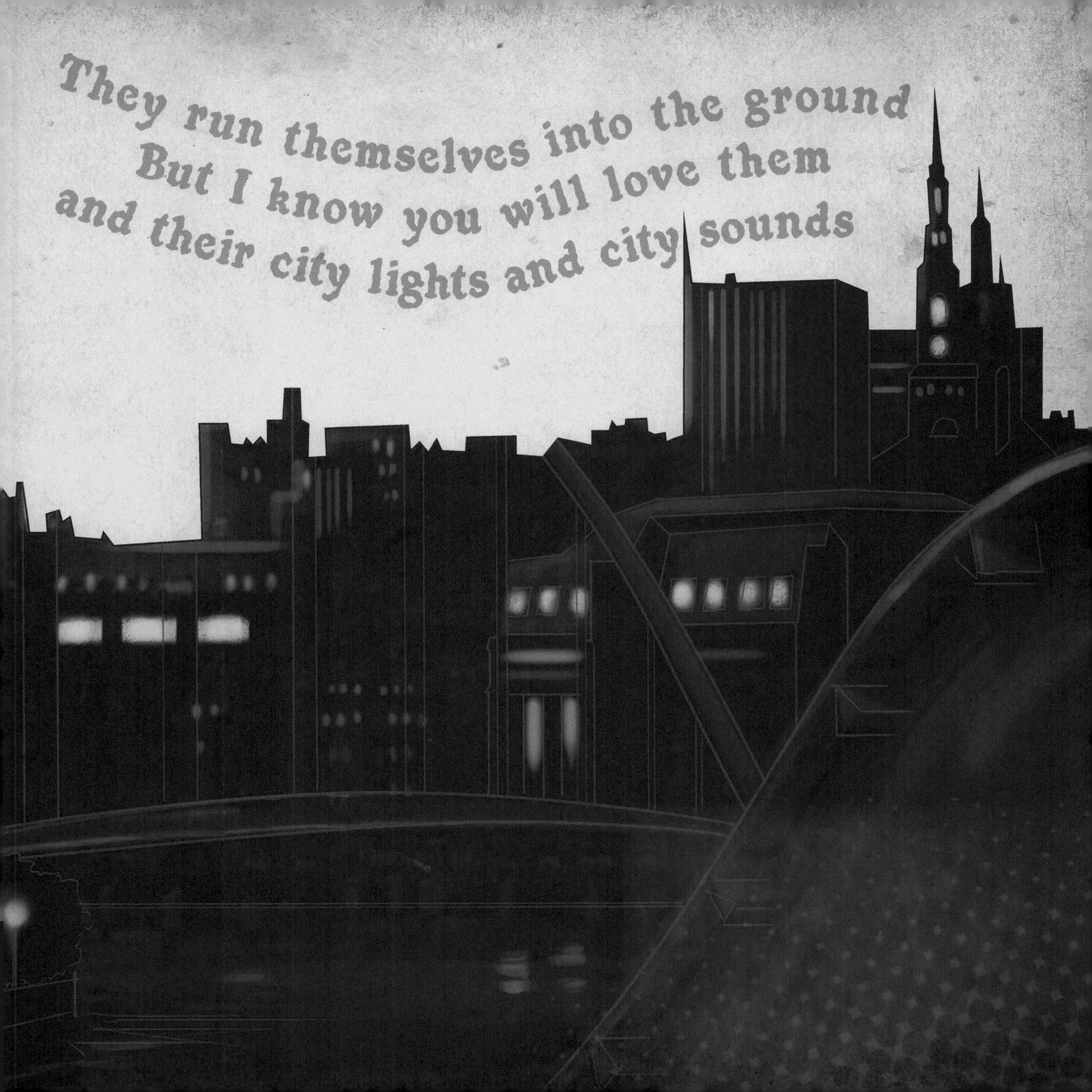

They run themselves into the ground
But I know you will love them
and their city lights and city sounds

THERE'S

BEAUTY

IN THE STRUGGLE

ANYTIME
I FEEL IT
GET ME
DOWN

I SEE YOU SMILING

Caroline, I'm on my way back home to you
Can't imagine what I'm going through
without you by my side
It's been a long, long time
Oh, won't you say a prayer for me?
I hope you will remember me
You're always on my mind, my Caroline
Oh, my Caroline

NOW, I HAVE
SEEN THINGS
IN THE SKY
STARS AND
LIGHTS AND
BIRDS
AND I

I'VE BEEN

ROCKY

MOUNTAIN HIGH

AND TOLD THEM ALL ABOUT YOU

Because you are still the only thing
that constantly amazes me

I love the road
and I've been blessed
but I love you best

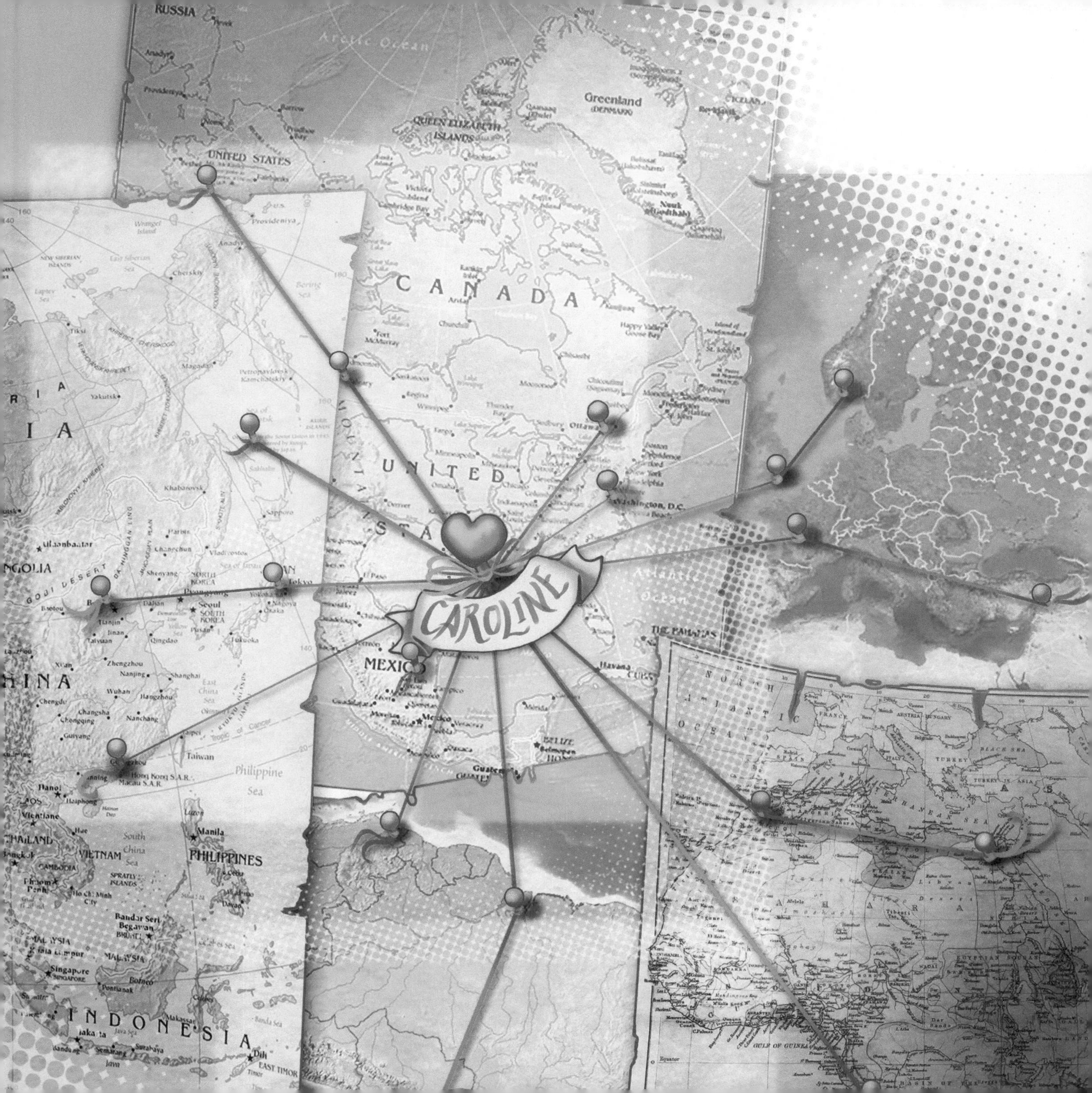

CAROLINE
RUSSIA
Arctic Ocean
Greenland
(DENMARK)
QUEEN ELIZABETH
ISLANDS
UNITED STATES
CANADA
UNITED
MEXICO
Havana
BELIZE
Atlantic
Ocean
NORTH
ATLANTIC
OCEAN
MONGOLIA
CHINA
GOBI DESERT
NORTH KOREA
SOUTH KOREA
Seoul
Taiwan
Philippine
Sea
Manila
PHILIPPINES
VIETNAM
THAILAND
CAMBODIA
South
China
Sea
Singapore
INDONESIA
EAST TIMOR
Hong Kong S.A.R.
Macau S.A.R.
Tokyo
Vladivostok
Khabarovsk
Ottawa
Washington, D.C.
Greenland
Anadyr
Providenya
Barrow
Fairbanks
Tropic of Cancer
GULF OF GUINEA

CAROLINE

CAROLINE,
I'M ON MY WAY BACK
HOME TO YOU
CAN'T IMAGINE
WHAT I'M GOIN' THROUGH
WITHOUT YOU
BY MY SIDE

IT'S BEEN A LONG,
LONG TIME

OH, WON'T YOU SAY
A PRAYER FOR ME

I HOPE YOU WILL REMEMBER ME

YOU'RE ALWAYS
ON MY MIND

YOU WERE
ALWAYS
ON MY MIND,

MY CAROLINE

THE END

Singer-songwriter Brandi Carlile has enjoyed over a decade of commerical and critical success. Inspired by her niece, Carlile wrote the lyrics to the song "Caroline" to express how much she missed her while on the road. Carlile lives in Washington state with her wife and her many farm animals . . . and her niece Caroline not too far away.

CPSIA information can be obtained
at www.ICGtesting.com
Printed in the USA
BVHW060458181221
624355BV00002B/30

* 9 7 8 0 9 8 3 8 1 2 0 7 4 *